Animal Builders

Susan Taylor

Contents

Animal Builders

Some animals are very good builders. They build homes so that they have a place to care for their babies. A home is somewhere for animals to keep food, too.

Beavers build their homes using wood.

Paper wasps build their nests from paper.

Some animals work in teams to build a home. The home is a safe place for them to live together.

Tent Caterpillars

Tent caterpillars are insects.
They live together in a **colony**.

In spring, tent caterpillars build a nest in a tree.
They make the nest from **silk** that they spin.
The nest looks like a little tent.

Tent caterpillars stay inside the nest
on very hot days and on days when it is raining.

Soon the caterpillars come out of the nest.
Then, they are ready to turn into moths.

Tent caterpillars turn into moths.

Paper Wasps

Paper wasps are insects.
These wasps live together in colonies.

Paper wasps build their nests from paper.

To make the paper, they chew **bark** from trees.
When the bark is soft and wet,
they put it on the nest.

When the bark is dry, it turns into paper.
The paper is thin, but it is very hard to break.

The paper nests are a safe home for baby wasps.

Termites

Termites are insects that live in colonies.
They work together to build a nest.
Some nests look like tall towers.

There are many rooms and tiny tunnels in the tower.
The termites are safe inside their nest.

Some termite nests look like towers.

Many termites live together inside the nest.

It can get very warm inside a termite nest.
The termites make holes at the top and sides
to let the hot air out.
This keeps the nest cool.

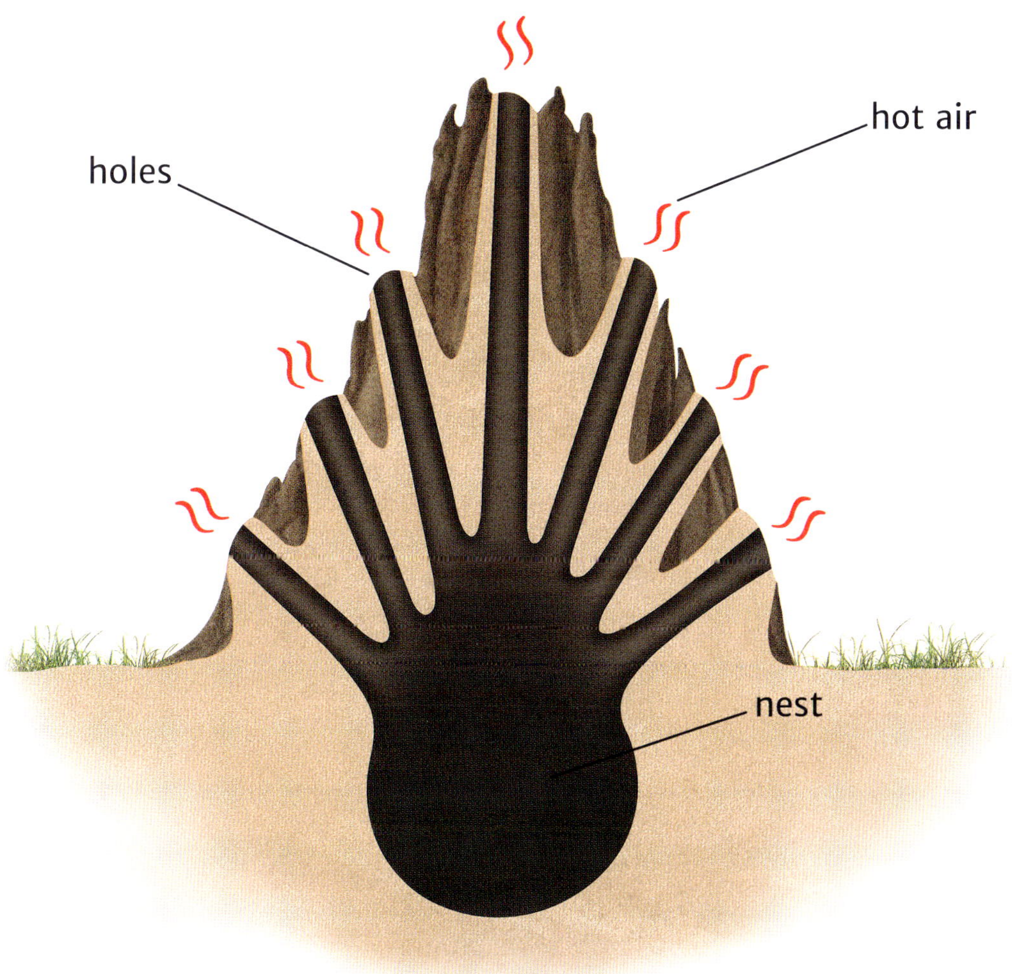

A termite nest has holes at the top and sides to let hot air out.

Weaver Birds

Weaver birds build nests that look like baskets. The nests are made from sticks and grass. There is a hole at the front of the nest so that the parents can fly in and out.

Weaver birds build their nests
in the branches of trees.

Some of the nests are very big and heavy.
Sometimes, the nests drop out of the tree
and onto the ground.

Beavers

Beavers are animals that live in rivers.
They build a home in the river, called a **lodge**.

A lodge is made from wood.
Beavers cut down trees with their sharp teeth.
They carry the wood to the river in their mouths.

Beavers hide from wolves and bears
in their lodges.

A beaver builds its lodge in a river.

Chimpanzees

Chimpanzees build nests in trees. They find tree branches in the forest. They break up the branches to make a nest to sleep in.

Chimpanzees can sleep safely in their nests, away from other animals.

Some animals are clever builders.
They carefully build homes and places to sleep.

Sometimes, animals work together
to build a home.
They keep themselves and their families safe
inside the home.

Glossary

bark (*noun*) the outside part of a tree or branch

colony (*noun*) insects that all live together in the same home

lodge (*noun*) the home a beaver builds using wood from trees

silk (*noun*) thin, strong string made by insects like spiders and caterpillars